'Challenging, clever [illegible] generations of Germans are sun[illegible] r of the last century.' —AMANDA CRAIG, *Independent*

'A book we should all be reading, so find a copy. It has been one of my reading experiences of the year.' —SIMON SAVIDGE, *Savidge Reads*

'This is an intelligent, acute and horrifically intense book. It didn't so much take my breath away as make me gasp for air.'
—SAM JORDISON, *The Observer* Books of the Year

Praise for *Clara's Daughter*

'The deftly arranged sequence of scenes gradually reveals the fears and needs of each protagonist and their relationships with each other, outlined with a careful, thoughtful style that creates an unusual atmosphere of charged bleakness. Strange, but oddly impressive.'
—HARRY RITCHIE, *Daily Mail*

'This searching, beautifully written novel gets to the heart of a woman's attempts to step out of the role of her mother's daughter, and make sense of the person she has become. Terrific.' —KATE SAUNDERS, *The Times*

Praise for *Kauthar*

'*Kauthar*, as much an exploration of breakdown and collapse as of the lines between devotion and delusion, faith and fundamentalism, does not shy away from suffering and darkness; instead, as in *Magda* and *Clara's Daughter*, Ziervogel goes bravely to the bleakest points of humanity and illuminates them with her lyrical and enthralling prose.'
—CLAIRE KOHDA, *The Guardian*

'Ziervogel writes with insight and fluency, articulating a profound empathy with those at the extreme reaches of their endurance. Searingly contemporary, *Kauthar* sketches out a humane and subtle counterpoint to the distorted debate surrounding religious radicalisation, and in doing so is resonant and timely.' —LETTIE KENNEDY, *The Observer*

Praise for *The Photographer*

'Two generations on from her own grandmother's experience, Ziervogel shines a humanising light into the dark spots of her country's history.' —LUCY ASH, *The Observer*

'Few books have the ability to move the reader in the first pages, as *The Photographer* does . . . Ziervogel makes us question ideas of innocence and blame during fraught times . . . [she] shows us the less visible effects of war, and the ways in which it can corrupt and change us.'
—CLAIRE KOHDA, *Times Literary Supplement*

Praise for *Flotsam*

'Ziervogel . . . grew up in Germany and this taut, mysterious novel not only conjures female subjectivities and grief, but it also paints a haunting portrait of the country in the 1950s, with its greater sense of loss, and the looming spectre of crimes committed during the war.'
—ARIFA AKBAR, *The Guardian*

'Anna's experience of World War Two and the consequences of an event in the war, dominates her daughter's life. *Flotsam* asks how will the next generation live in the shadow of such destruction, when so much of that history is left silent? Wonderfully concise yet powerful, *Flotsam* seems simple while offering a layered intelligence that should be valued.'
—JAMES DOYLE, *Bookmunch*

Meike Ziervogel is the author of six novels. She founded an award-winning publishing house in the UK, Peirene Press, and co-founded Alsama Project, an innovative NGO providing secondary education in refugee camps in the Middle East.

ALSO BY MEIKE ZIERVOGEL

Magda
Clara's Daughter
Kauthar
The Photographer
Flotsam

MEIKE
ZIERVOGEL

SHAMS

CROMER

PUBLISHED BY SALT PUBLISHING 2025

2 4 6 8 10 9 7 5 3 1

First published in Great Britain in 2025 by
Salt Publishing Ltd
12 Norwich Road, Cromer, Norfolk NR27 0AX, United Kingdom

www.saltpublishing.com

Salt Publishing Limited Reg. No. 5293401

A CIP catalogue record for this book is available from the British Library

ISBN 978 1 78463 348 6 (Paperback edition)
ISBN 978 1 78463 349 3 (Electronic edition)

Typeset in Neacademia by Salt Publishing

Printed and bound in Great Britain by Clays Ltd, Elcograf S.p.A.

To the Alsama students

لن تستطيعي أن تجدي الشمس في غرفة مغلقة
You can't find the sun in a locked room.

—GHASSAN KANAFANI

Note: the Arabic word for 'sun' is شمس / shams

PART ONE

1

OUTSIDE, in the city, life begins early, between four and five in the morning. That's usually when she goes to sleep, and she doesn't stir until well into late morning, more like around noon. She's getting on now, in her eighth decade. She shouldn't really be here anymore – her type isn't meant to survive for more than a few years. But recently she's been kept busy, she's in demand. Her folds have become deeper and darker, more dangerous. Though also softer. Whoever comes, she takes them in, puts her huge arms around them and pulls them close, towards her belly. And there they then lie, like babies, like lovers – men and women and children, old and young and newborns. Some fall asleep straight away, surrendering to her oozing, sweet-sour stink. Others suck her nipples, play with her breasts, explore her folds with their tongues, their fingers, their penises. She lets them. It's their right. Eventually they all fall asleep. And that's what she's waiting for. Then she draws them even closer, right inside her, and curls up around them, and buries her nose in their hair, and rocks them gently, ever so gently, from side to side, humming quietly, no particular tune, a mix of Umm Kulthum and Fairuz and Amr Diab and Fares Karam and the call to prayer. Her children, she gathers them up, she loves them all and she protects them. She strokes heads and absorbs fears and nightmares, screams and tears. She lets them rage against themselves and against the world, and if they harm themselves and others, what does it matter? She loves and forgives and lullabies them into a beautiful sleep. Forgetting and escape, these are what she offers.

She likes to imagine herself as a big fat mother, one of those ancient fertility goddess figurines, usually crouching, with a belly that has many folds and with massive heavy tits hanging down, eternally filled with nourishing sweet milk for all her thousands and thousands of babies. Her hips sway when she walks, and her folds swing, and her thighs rub against each other and her laugh covers the earth.

She's a shapeshifter. What she imagines, she is. Yet at a blink of an eye her true nature appears. All wires and vessels and tubes and tendons and sinews and cancerous growths and brittle bones turning increasingly crooked by the day are there for everyone to see. Her skin, deprived of the sun for decades, has become so thin and transparent that it might as well not exist. She pees and shits in the narrow alleyways, self-respect a word without meaning. And with the thunderstorms in winter her watery embrace becomes deadly, while the lightning that charges through her veins electrocutes whoever dares touch her.

Shatila is her name. One of the oldest refugee camps on earth. In Arabic the word means 'justice' and 'insight'. She runs the best whorehouse in town. You can get women, and girls and boys, and body parts and weapons and drugs. If you pay, you get. And no one bothers you. In her house, she alone is the law. She will protect you from the forces outside and rock you to sleep. But the house rules are tough. You might be raped or robbed or kidnapped. Tough luck. Do not complain. That is the deal. Just come and crawl into her arms and she will sing you to sleep.

The older she grows, the more alluring she becomes. Travellers arrive from afar looking for a thrill, a kick, wanting to touch her for just a moment, to lay their eyes on her. Others study her, write theses about her. Sometimes they stay for a week, sometimes for a month, but rarely longer. Danger and ugliness and evil reside within her. If you don't have to stay, you leave.

2

'I'LL come back for you,' Omar says.

Of course he says it. And in that moment, he believes what he says, and Shams believes him too. After all, they are young.

They stand huddled against the dilapidated wall inside the scrapyard on the edge of the camp. To their left and right lean big rusty red-orange and purple-brown sheets of metal. Someone, probably the profoundly deaf who guards the yard after hours and earns a good income on the side by providing a secret spot for lovers, has pushed the sheets aside so that the thumping noise couples might produce against the wall will not be heard. The call for the Maghrib prayer has just begun, but Omar and Shams aren't the first this evening. Omar kicked a used condom to the side, hoping that Shams wouldn't notice. But she did notice. And anyway, she knows what she wants. She'd furtively pressed an extra five thousand into the hand of the old man once Omar had already turned inside the yard, to buy them a few more minutes.

With a slow, deliberate movement, Shams now pulls her hijab back. She has come prepared, wearing it more loosely, with no underscarf. She releases the big hairpin, her thick black hair uncurling to the bottom of her spine. Many times she has practised for this moment, imagining the situation in front of the small mirror above the kitchen sink in the early morning when everyone else is still asleep. Now, it has the desired effect.

'You are beautiful,' Omar gasps, running his fingers gently through her soft hair, then twisting it around his hand and bringing it up to his nose, inhaling the rose oil. The acrid smell of the scrapyard vanishes from his senses.

For a moment Shams's eyes remain open, taking in the yard. Pipes and dismantled cars and old washing machines and broken fans. Machine junk looking like slaughtered aliens. An iron taste is settling on her tongue. She closes her eyes. Their lips touch. They kiss. She wants more, so much more. Omar will save her from this inhuman world. He will take her to Norway. With him by her side she will become happy. She already knows that she doesn't want to live without him ever again. In her eyes he is already her husband.

And she needs to be quick about choosing her own husband. Otherwise, her aunt will do it for her.

'Fadel has asked for your hand and I have agreed,' Shams's uncle announced a few weeks ago.

Shams has lived with her uncle and aunt in the camp for as long as she can remember. Back in Syria she used to have a father and a mother and two brothers. Now Shams's family do not even visit her in her dreams.

Fadel is a cousin on her aunt's side. He is ugly and dim-witted and fat. And old: thirty-something.

Shams was not surprised. She had expected her aunt to start bringing her suitors. Most girls in the camp are married off at around her age, sometimes even younger. Sheima, her best friend, is now married and already pregnant, and Afifa, one of her second cousins who Shams likes even though the girl is three years younger, can't stop talking about getting engaged soon.

Early marriage eases the burden on the family as there's one less mouth to feed, and also earns them some money, while at the same time, if the man comes from the same clan, the girls and the money stays within the tribe. What's more, the teenagers themselves want it. It's the only way they can have sex without bringing shame on their family.

Shams heard herself say, 'My mother would have wanted me to finish my education.'

~

Shams's mother had been allowed to go to school, while her older sister, Umm Ali, never even learned to read and write. Umm Ali and Abu Ali are both illiterate and before the war had never left their village.

If Shams had already known Omar when her aunt suggested Fadel, she would have said, 'I'm in love with Omar and I will marry him. He's travelling with his family to Norway and when I'm eighteen I will go and live with him there. In Norway all girls go to school, even if they are married. Afterwards I will go to university and become a lawyer to fight for the rights of girls around the world. And you can't stop me.'

Shams's uncle jumped up, raising his hand to hit the girl who managed to duck, taking a step back. Umm Ali grabbed her husband by the shirt, pulling him back down onto the mattress where they were sitting. Shams had just served her uncle and aunt tea, and they were sharing a shisha.

'I'll talk to her,' Umm Ali said, smoke rising from her mouth. She gave her husband a light push on the shoulder to encourage him to leave the room.

'You are no longer safe here,' Umm Ali said when he had gone, looking her niece straight in the eyes. 'You are a girl of marriageable age. Men have begun to notice you.'

'You mean my cousins.' Shams's words were barely audible but she couldn't speak louder without betraying the tremble in her voice. 'They have noticed me for a while,' she continued, 'and it's never seemed to bother you.'

Five of Umm Ali's youngest children are still living at home, including two teenage boys, everyone sleeping together in one room. Ahmed tried to rape Shams from behind one night, but she had noticed his glances for weeks and been prepared. She put a knife to his throat and when he offered her money if she let him finish what he wanted to do – after all, it was from behind and would leave her a virgin – she had pressed the knife ever so slightly into the skin of his neck until a little red dot appeared.

'You will bring shame on this family,' her aunt now insisted.

Shams shook her head.

'That's not under your control,' Umm Ali pointed out.

'If a man forces himself on me against my will, it's called rape. There is no shame in it.'

The last sentence was said so quietly that it came out of her mouth as barely a whisper. Because according to the law of the camp, and to the traditions and customs of her aunt and uncle, rape has no meaning. It is all about honour – the honour of the family, the clan, the tribe.

Shams is now pushing herself against Omar, holding him tight. She desires him. And if he does what she wants him to do, she will be his forever.

3

MY body is heavy and I don't like to move. When I do move, it's slowly. Sleeping is the best, dozing on the mattress with the TV glimmering at a low level. I'm a woman who has done her duty. I've given birth to eleven children. Praise be to God.

There is barely any natural light coming into our place. It makes me feel as if I'm living deep inside the earth or at the bottom of the ocean. It makes me feel safe.

I don't like to go out. It's not good for my knees going up and down those narrow stairs. The steps are so uneven, made of clay with a few loose tiles stuck on top. There are no railings and it's full of rubbish from the plastic bags that are dumped outside the apartment doors and ripped open by rats and cats. Going down is almost as hard, if not harder, than coming up. Going down I have to be so careful where I tread, and I have to turn my feet slightly sideways because the steps are so small. I'm always scared I will slip.

When I wake up in the late morning I like Shams to bathe my feet and massage them. I will miss her. But my boys have their urges – after all, they are young men. And she too is becoming hungry. I can see it in her eyes. She needs to go, and Fadel is as good as anyone. She will still be able to come round and we can sit together and watch TV. It's scary, what's happening outside in the city. Demonstrations and burning tyres and smouldering rubbish heaps and flaming mountains from the heat. Inside here we are safe. They look after us. Shatila looks after us.

4

THE twenty-first century is a glorious era for Shatila. She is multiplying across the planet as never before. Refugee camps are springing up everywhere, right in the middle of cities. They contain Palestinians and Syrians and Yemenis, Somalis and Rwandans and Afghans, an ever-increasing number of nationalities.

Like Shatila herself, her offspring are not marked on maps as refugee camps, but everyone knows where they are. Those who go inside rarely come out again. The camps are black holes. No walls or fences surround them. No need. Fear serves as an effective barrier. People living inside the camps have no rights outside. They have no passports, no residency or work permits, no health insurance, no bank accounts and often not even a birth certificate; they cannot vote. These people do not exist. Moreover, there are no benevolent authorities administering the camps. Governments everywhere have washed their hands of these places because officially the refugees living inside the camps don't exist and therefore, of course, officially, the camps don't exist. So these places are self-governing, or in other words they are controlled by drug lords, warlords and weapons dealers. No regulations concerning building, sanitation or rubbish collection are ever imposed. And there are no laws limiting the number of inhabitants. Those who enter a black hole disappear. Yet, the areas of the camps can't expand, originally intended for three thousand people, they often end up providing refuge for forty thousand or more. The land and houses are privately owned, so landlords and owners get richer by the year as they build ever more floors arbitrarily on top of each other, demanding rent from the refugees, who, of course, don't have the money and so have to monetize what little they call their own – their children and their dignity.

Alleyways become so narrow that only one slim person can walk along them at a time. Houses are built so close to each other that there is hardly a hand's width between them. The dwellings themselves are tiny. One room for an entire extended family, plus a small kitchen area barely large enough for a sink, fridge and two-hob cooker, and an even tinier bathroom just about suitable for a toilet and a shower head fixed to the wall above it. A foldable plastic contraption divides kitchen and bathroom because there is no space for a proper door. Also, windows are scarce because it would cost the landlord money to install them. Occasionally there is a small opening in the kitchen, but really it doesn't matter, as daylight and a fresh breeze wouldn't be able to force their way in. Even the alleyways rarely see the sun, with the walls reaching so high and an impenetrable web of intertwining electric wires and water pipes running between them.

Naturally, these camps are heaven for charities and do-gooders. NGOs run education projects: a few months of English classes here, of literacy and 'awareness' classes there, occasionally even IT skills. Some children, especially the girls – Shams among them – grab every opportunity. They sign up for each course, arrive on time, always with a pen and a notebook at the ready, always with their homework done. It isn't clear what they want to do with their education. What are they thinking? They can never escape the camp. Yet they are like addicts. Education – what it does to their brain, to their imagination – gives them a buzz, a high.

And they are relentless in their pursuit of it. They rise early every morning, before anyone else, and you see them hurrying along the narrow, empty alleyways, to be at the doors of the charity centres half an hour before they open. Even though, nothing more than tiny educational morsels is ever thrown their way – three months here, six months there.

~

'*Alhamdulillah,*' Shatila sighs. After all, she herself is not keen on sustainable education. It might endanger her very existence. It might change the neural pathways in the brains of these little creatures. They might start organizing their thoughts, structuring their days, fighting the lethargy that hopelessness plants in their bones. And what would happen then to Shatila's alleyways? Would they begin to clean them up, maybe put flowerpots everywhere, sort out rules and regulations for where to run the electric wiring and the water pipes? Develop their own ideas, desires, plans? Ask landlords to put windows into each room? To plaster the walls? To repair the blocked drains? Maybe to forbid the carrying of guns in public? Even the owning of guns? And to choose their own lovers? The possibilities are frightening.

But unrealistic.

Because no one wants that to happen. Not Shatila, not the country, not the world. Not the mothers. Not the fathers. Not the young men and the boys. They love to show off, with guns tucked in the back of their trousers, racing through the alleyways on their mopeds.

And so a few limited educational morsels continue to be dropped haphazardly throughout the camp, to keep up the appearance that refugee education is a serious undertaking. Of course, occasionally the odd girl succeeds in picking up every single morsel before the rats can get to them, diligent little creature that she is. And she begins to string the morsels together like glass beads to make a necklace. And then she wears this ridiculous, useless necklace for everyone to see, and rushes through the alleyways with shiny eyes and red cheeks, her wild imagination solidifying into a tangible, executable plan.

5

'MARRY me.' Shams's lips move on top of Omar's while her hands slide down to his waist and start to fumble with his trouser zip.

When words didn't help to convince her aunt, Shams lay down on the mattress, exactly where she had been sitting. She curled up into a ball and faced the wall. Talking to her aunt and uncle wouldn't get her anywhere. From now on, she would simply refuse to move as long as they insisted that she marry Cousin Fadel.

Twelve hours passed. She didn't move. Twenty-four hours passed. She still didn't move.

Umm Ali screamed that Shams had brought a curse on the family, letting her fists rain down on the girl. Shams didn't move. She had fought worse monsters.

The neighbours came and pulled Umm Ali away from her niece.

'Leave her. The girl will come to her senses. Eventually, they all do. We did too.'

After Shams had successfully refused to marry Cousin Fadel, something inside her stirred.

Yes, they all hissed behind her back:

'Shame on you. You will bring damnation on your family.'

'You will die an old spinster.'

'You will go mad like your mother, who thought she was above us all just because she went to school. She chose her own husband and look what happened.'

'You are already as mad as your mother.'

'Someone will take you by force and then you'll have to marry him and your bastard child will be cursed.'

So Shams began avoiding the darkest alleyways, and there were a couple of times when she thought she heard someone behind her and raced back home. Yet despite her fears and sometimes a tiny regret that she didn't marry Fadel, because maybe she should have, because maybe that's just how things are meant to be and it would have got her out of her aunt's house, Shams began to feel a solidity about herself, a focus within herself, her own presence in the world. And this presence, her presence, could move forward the way she willed it to move.

For a few seconds Omar's hands are still on her shoulders. Then suddenly he lifts them, taking a step away from her, but not so far that her hands can no longer reach him.

'Please stop. I'll come back' – he is breathing heavily – 'then we get married.'

For a moment Shams's fingers cease to move. But she keeps them on his trousers.

'Prove it,' she says. 'Now.'

She doesn't care what will happen once they move out of the shadows of the scrapyard, once she has to wave Omar goodbye. The goodbye is still a lifetime away. A different world. And whatever will happen in this other world, the next world, her next life, the life beyond this very moment, she will be able to survive, to live, only if she is with him. Now. And forever.

PART TWO

6

AT first it is only a tiny flickering flame in the far distance and she isn't sure that the oxygen available will be enough for the flame to survive. Yet it keeps on approaching, and all of a sudden it begins to shine a glorious bright light on her. And Shatila appears as what she has always been: a goddess, protective of those who obey her rules; unforgiving towards those who betray her. Who try to outwit her . . . to destroy her . . . who do not bow to her. She smells the messenger, the chosen one, the one who will be her knight in shining armour, arriving from afar. Oh, the stench of greed and self-interest precedes him – she inhales it, she inhales him. Come, my little lover boy, come into Mama's arms. You are perfect. There is little I have to teach you. You will be my loyal servant and your rewards will be plentiful.

Shatila quivers with a sexual excitement she hasn't felt in years. She will make him wild with lust for her, the beautiful young goddess with soft, smooth, milk-coloured skin and emerald-green eyes through which you can see to the very bottom of the oceans. And her limbs, tender and slim and firm. She will wrap her legs around him and never let him go. Oh, what a find. Come closer, come closer . . . You will be my saviour.

He doesn't yet know what he is capable of. What man does, until he is touched? But he has always had a sense that he was chosen for something special.

She will take his hands and guide them deep into her folds, her big wobbly folds, and she will feed him on her hanging breasts, her used-up tits where thousands and thousands have suckled, and if ever he were to look up he would see her true face, a Medusa head with snakes crawling all over it and dead eyes that turn you to stone. But he won't look up. He's too busy fucking her. This is his chance. He is the benevolent one, the one who will lead mankind to a glorious future. And the world is praying to him and worshipping him, and he is guiding them because he is the one who knows.

The burden is heavy. Sometimes he feels he's breaking under the weight and the loneliness threatens to devour him.

She strokes his damp hair. Poor little darling, you've already exhausted yourself. But he has far more strength in him. He is Shatila's right hand, her tool. With him on her side, she will live forever.

7

WHEN I first began working in the camp, I was full of ideas, of common sense and goodwill. For example, I wanted to turn the camp green. I began conversations with landscape architects, experts at growing gardens up the sides of concrete tower blocks.

Since this would have required some time to set up – we needed to get more funding first, before the actual growing of the plants could start – I had another idea. We distributed earth and seeds to as many households as possible, then we taught them how to make flower beds and trellises out of the plastic water bottles that litter the alleyways. Afterwards we encouraged competition: whoever had the fastest-growing plants would receive more earth and more seeds. In my mind's eye I already saw a beautiful green camp with beanstalks and tomato plants on every balcony and window ledge, with sweet peas adding colour and scent. I also planned a whole cycle of neighbourhood workshops on sustainable urban gardening and nature reserves. My plan was to explain that green spaces make us happier, lighter, calmer and even healthier. And that asthma cases would reduce dramatically.

But the project never got off the ground. In fact it fell at the first hurdle.

I had of course expected problems. At the outset of the project, I didn't know where these problems would come from and what they would look like – after all, one never knows. Any new endeavour is bound to face problems. With my green camp it was the salt water. The water that comes out of the taps in the camp, into every bathroom and kitchen, is taken straight from the sea. At the beginning that didn't stop me. It was a challenge that I was happy – no, excited – to take on. So what? I thought. We will simply change to plants that can tolerate salt water. In addition, the camp has very little natural light. Humidity in the summer is extremely high and in the winter the camp is half under water anyway. So it lies at the bottom of the sea, I thought to myself. Wasn't this our chance to turn it into a stunning coral reef, with the inhabitants like happy shoals of fish swarming around it, feeding off it? I began to research, eager to learn more. In addition, I reached out to environmentalists to see if new plants could be cultivated that would thrive on salt water. I saw the water issue as a challenge, but certainly not as an insurmountable problem.

And at the beginning it was just that, an exciting yet surely surmountable challenge. We succeeded in persuading a few households to begin growing plants and to attend the first saltwater-plant workshop. I remember in particular Umm Ali and her husband, Abu Ali. When I first met her, I thought she must be in her seventies at least: such a wrinkled, yellow face, with black shadows under her hollow eyes, wearing a black abaya and black hijab, bent over with a limp. Maybe two months passed. Then her first plants started growing and suddenly a new woman turned up at the workshop. At first, I didn't recognize her. Energetic stride, open face, green hijab with yellow flowers. Her sparkling eyes were a beautiful light brown. She told us how she talked to the plants each morning, telling them all her worries. And the plants liked the fact that she talked to them, and they were growing very fast, and they calmed her down. Even Abu Ali had noticed how lovely his wife was now. And she giggled like a teenage girl in love.

But then calamity struck. Mosquitoes and other biting insects apparently descended on the camp. I say 'apparently' because I never got stung. But it was all blamed on the plants. Umm Ali was the first to turn up at our office with her husband in tow. She made him lift his trouser leg to reveal a white, old man's leg scratched bloody in numerous places.

'It's from the plants, everyone tells me,' she said, and continued in a shrill, accusing voice to inform us that she'd got rid of them, all of them, because their landlord, Mustafa the Tough, had come round with a gun and said he would throw her out unless she pulled out the plants immediately.

She was angry with us. She accused us in a torrent of words and unstructured thoughts of exploiting her with our fancy Western-influenced ideas. That's what Umm Khalid, her friend, had explained to her. That this growing of plants everywhere was a colonizing idea, to do with wanting to rule everything, and that's not how Muslims live. 'We come from the desert,' she said. And she needed some medicine for her husband, and she had no money, and everyone said we should have paid her anyway for growing these plants and she felt exploited and everyone said our NGO was no good.

And then she broke down in sobs.

She was defending us, yes she was, she insisted. But now her husband's condition had got worse and maybe he would die.

All the while, her husband stared at a spot on the floor in front of him. His hands were resting flat on his knees, ready to push down so he could stand up and leave when his wife had finally finished her performance.

I knew that the plants had nothing to do with her husband's condition. I also doubted that her husband's bloody leg had anything to do with the plants. Yet eventually I pulled out of my pocket the twenty-dollar note I had stuffed into it that morning when I found it in front of the mirror in my hallway, where it must have fallen the previous day while I rummaged in my trouser pocket for my mobile.

I gave her the money to shut her up, to get her out of my office, to ease my guilt. My guilt for wanting to get her out of my office. I needed to think, to try and figure out if I was guilty of colonizing. Me? An Arab poet wanting to colonize my own people? It was laughable, ridiculous. But the more I went inside myself and thought, the more I had to admit that for this poor woman the fear was probably real. What did I really know about life as a stateless refugee biding my time in a camp?

That evening, as I was lying on my bed, panic suddenly gripped me by the throat. I was disgusted with myself. What was I trying to achieve with my fancy ideas? Did I really think that these poor refugees could be saved by urban plants when they didn't even have access to basic services such as clean water?

What right – yes, what Umm Ali had said was true – what right did I have to invade their space and tell them how to live? I had no right, because it was of no benefit to them. And suddenly it struck me: this doing-good was all about me and nothing to do with others.

To help the refugees, I had to begin to see the world through their eyes, to use their traditional value systems.

8

THERE is a notice stuck to the classroom wall. The organization that is running the three-month gender equality project which Shams is currently attending is looking for a cleaner. Applicants must be eighteen or over.

Without hesitation Shams adds a year to her age and puts her name down. If she were to bring home a weekly contribution to the household, it would be more difficult for her aunt to insist she get married.

The job is cleaning Mr Tony's apartment once a week. Mr Tony is the boss of the charity. He is well known in the camp because they don't just run educational projects on gender equality, they also distribute food boxes and give cash assistance. Shams tells her aunt and uncle that the job is at the organization's headquarters. They would never allow her to go to a single man's apartment.

She is picked up by a taxi outside the camp and driven to a lovely airy place on a fourth floor in a nice-looking area.

Yet it isn't the sea view that takes Shams's breath away. It's the shelves filled with books upon books upon books - hundreds of them, in Arabic and English and - another language that she will soon learn - French. Carefully, scared to break the books and their spell, Shams runs her fingertips along their spines.

Mr Tony is never at home when Shams comes to clean. She picks up the key from the concierge on the ground floor, then drops it back when she has finished. She would love to touch the books, take them out, maybe even try to read one of them. But she is too nervous. What if she isn't allowed to? And even if she pulls out just one book, perhaps it will show afterwards because she might not manage to return it to exactly the same place. Maybe the books are all secretly marked in their spots. And if she moves them without permission danger might be unleashed.

~

I can't see the monster. But I know it is there. It hurts Mum. But Mum is clever. She lies very still. I've spent a lot of time in the darkened room by my mother's side, watching over her. Making sure she is still breathing. Sometimes I'm scared that Mum is dead. I used to nudge her but then she would groan in pain. Now I have become more grown-up and I wait to see if the blanket moves. I have become very good at not blinking. Because if I blink I might miss the movement.

I've asked Mum what it looks like. But she just says, 'What monster?'

That's the problem: as soon as the monster has disappeared, Mum forgets about it. As if it never existed. But while it is there, of course I can't talk to her about it because then the monster would know where Mum is hiding and would launch an even fiercer attack.

Sometimes, sitting in Mum's room, I forget the monster. And I just enjoy the light summer breeze that smells of sweet jasmine coming in through the opening where the curtains don't close properly. Occasionally a single white petal is blown into the room. I can hear the mosque and from further away some church bells. The juice vendor passes by with the cling-cling of the shallow brass bowls he holds in his hand and the tinkle-tinkle of the many coins hanging from chains fastened to the large metal tank that is slung on his back. And then there is the '*Ma'dan, ma'dan, nhas, hadid, tanak*' ('Metals, metals, copper, iron, cans') of the metal buyers who drive into our neighbourhood and stand at the back of their open trucks. And when the coffee seller comes by with his cart, a rich roasty smell reminds me of my *teta*, my grandmother. Then I feel very warm in my tummy and can't imagine that there are any monsters in the world at all.

Still, here is what I figured: the monster is dangerous and hurts Mum a lot, but I don't think it wants to kill her. It needs Mum. It has attacked Mum for as long as I can remember. Recently it's become even more aggressive, the assaults more frequent. I find it hard to keep up with my homework because I spend a lot of time watching over Mum, and at school I can't concentrate because I keep on thinking about what the monster might do.

Mum says she suffers from something called *migraine*. Dad says it has got worse because of the 'situation'.

~

Shams puts the key into the lock and the door springs open straight away. For a split second she is surprised as it is usually double-locked. Then she steps inside and closes the door with a push. The *marhaba* – hello – comes unexpectedly. She swings around, automatically gripping the key like a knife ready in self-defence. A figure is getting up from the armchair in front of the open balcony doors, through which sunlight is pouring into the apartment. The figure is human in form, but faceless, only its shadowy contours visible against the light.

The shadow is walking towards her.

Feeling the metal of the key in her right hand, Shams steps backwards, lifting her free hand to search surreptitiously for the door handle.

The figure stops advancing.

~

One day I found my mum lying on the bathroom floor. I had got up in the middle of the night to go for a pee. I didn't turn on the light. I never turn on the light at night. And I also don't open my eyes fully. I know where everything is. After peeing I turned towards the sink and there my foot kicked against something. I shrieked.

'It's OK, Shams. It's me, *ya Mama*,' I heard her say in a weak voice.

I fumbled for the switch and turned the light on. She was lying on the floor curled up into a ball, hiding her head inside her elbows.

'Turn it off,' she whined in pain even before I had time to move my hand away from the switch.

I dropped to the floor and snuggled up close to her and put my arm around her.

'Go back to bed.'

I didn't want to go back to bed. How could I?

'Mum, come to bed.' I tried to pull her by the arm.

'Just leave me, will you? It's nice and cool here. I want to lie here for a while.'

It was freezing. My feet and hands were like ice.

And suddenly I understood: Mum was scared about going back into her bedroom. It was then that I realized I would have to deal with the monster.

I left the bathroom because Mum had asked me to. But I sat outside the door for the rest of the night.

~

'I'm sorry. It didn't mean to frighten you. I'm Mr Tony. Didn't the concierge tell you that I would be here today? I asked her to let you know.'

Shams's palm touches the door handle. She curls her fingers around it but doesn't yet press it down. The voice is pleasant.

She shakes her head. 'No, I wasn't told.'

'Oh,' Mr Tony responds. 'Do you mind if I'm here today? I won't be in your way. I will just sit in the chair and write my speech.'

She again shakes her head. 'It's OK.'

She likes it that he has asked her if she minds. No one has ever asked her permission before.

Shams still can't see anything except his outline. She lets go of the door handle behind her back and walks carefully into the room, heading towards where she always drops the key and her bag on a small table underneath a wall mirror. She keeps him in view, though, hoping to see more of his face.

She has always imagined Mr Tony to be tall, muscly, square-jawed. A princely knight saving refugees. Instead, from what she can tell so far, he is fairly small and thin, with rounded, drooping shoulders.

When she is eventually able to see his face, it suits his body. Pale and oval. Nothing handsome. Nothing knightly. Nothing manly. And nothing at all scary.

'By the way, I hope you have started examining my bookshelves,' he says, with a sweeping hand movement in the direction of the wall with the books. 'Feel free to borrow any book you like. I have thousands.'

'Thank you,' she replies, all of a sudden overcome by shyness. 'But there are so many. I wouldn't know where to start.'

Mr Tony walks over to the bookshelf and pulls one out.

'Why don't you start with this?' He turns towards her with the book in his outstretched hand. 'It's a story called *Al-Muhakama, The Trial*. One of my favourite books.'

And then he smiles. And it is as if the rays of sun that until only a few moments ago were gathered behind him on the balcony have all been bundled inside him and are beaming out. Towards her. Towards Shams. And only for her. And especially for her. Just her . . . bathing her in his beautiful light.

When she talks to Omar on WhatsApp in the evening, Shams wants to tell him about the smile but she knows he would misunderstand. He would get jealous, thinking she's in love with Mr Tony. How could she explain that this was not a lover smiling at her, not even a father, but . . . but . . . a god. She certainly can't say that to Omar. She hardly dares think it. And Omar has become so religious since he arrived in Norway. He now prays five times a day and has grown a beard. He hates the Norwegians, he says. They are *kuffar*, unbelievers. Sinning. Drinking and whoring and swearing. She would like to remind him that they too had sinned. Yet she always keeps quiet.

At the beginning there was lots of love in their talking. In fact, all their talking was about love, how much they missed each other, how beautiful she was looking. That he wanted to touch her again, that he couldn't wait till he was holding her in his arms once more. His talk was so full of love and desire and longing for her that there was never any time to talk about his new home, his new life in Norway. Eventually she became more insistent about asking questions. After all, she wanted to know, so she could prepare for when she joined him. But Omar avoided answering the questions, saying that he'd rather think about the future when they would be together. Then suddenly, maybe nine or ten months after he had left the camp, about half a year ago, he began telling her how much he hated the Norwegians. He told her that the Norwegian government wouldn't allow him to work unless he could speak the language first. But he hates the language, he says, that's why his brain refuses to learn it. It's a stupid, useless language, only spoken by *kuffar*. So now he has found some Arab friends and he spends all his time with them at the mosque.

He has also stopped talking about how it will be when she comes to live with him.

Today, for the first time, she doesn't mind. Indeed, she suddenly realizes that she no longer wants to go to Norway and live with Omar. As if Mr Tony's smile has shown her a new path: she will read all the books in his library.

~

You can't chop off the head of an invisible monster or shoot it or put a knife through its heart, unless you *know* it's there in front of you. There is only one way: I have to draw its attention to me first, in order to figure out what or who it is, and then I will eventually be able to kill it.

I blindfold myself, simulating the fact that I can't see the monster. I ask Thaer, my older brother, to punch me. He doesn't like the idea.

'Shams, you are a girl,' he says. 'I can't punch girls.'

'I'm your sister who you often don't like,' I correct him.

I also promise him that I will persuade Dad to take us to the Bakdash ice-cream men in Hamidiyah. Thaer loves the rose-and-almond-flavoured *bouza*.

'I'm not going to defend myself,' I reassure him.

Thaer places a light blow against my right upper arm.

'Harder.'

'How hard?'

'As hard as you like.'

I am not allowed to hit back. That's what I have told myself. I'd only scare Thaer and he'd stop practising with me. Thaer is one year older than me, but weak.

A few tentative hits. I call out where they are supposed to land: 'Right upper arm, right upper arm, left front leg, bum.'

'Which side?' Thaer asks. He is beginning to get into it.

'Left.'

The next punches come harder, more real. I clench my teeth.

'OK. Now next exercise. You call out where you're going to hit me and I have to catch your wrist before the punch lands.'

Our training sessions become longer. I get stronger. He throws me to the ground. I have to anticipate the next hook, fist throw, flat-hand karate blow. He begins to use his legs and feet. I have to be ready to be attacked from all sides.

Then, one day, Thaer doesn't manage to land a single punch. I anticipate them all. He becomes very frustrated, socking me harder, more frantically, furious that he can't get to me any longer, especially me, his little sister. We fight silently, without mercy. All the while I am not allowed to avenge myself, to hit out.

By now I have twice persuaded my father to take us to the Bakdash ice-cream parlour, and one Sunday we go on a trip to the almond forest in the mountains and sit by the river, where my parents smoke shisha and drink Almaza beer and we eat *shish taouk* with the yoghurt sauce running down our hands and onto our legs. And in a week or two my father will take us all for an evening picnic up on Mount Qasioun to watch the lights go on across the city. Thaer loves eating out and so he sees these trips as adequate compensation for his efforts in preparing me for the monster fight. (Of course, I still haven't told him that this is my goal.)

My training isn't yet complete, though. I know my brother too well, know the sequences in which he will hit. I must get used to different body shapes. The bigger and heavier the better.

I start with boys from my class, then move on to the older ones. By the time I am ready to face the big boys the fights have become famous. They take place underneath the old fig trees in the small park at the end of our school road.

That is, until Ustath Nabil, the English teacher, catches us.

At the beginning it was just my brother, who now always served as referee, myself and the boys who were chosen to fight me. I swore them to secrecy, as I did with my brother. But that only worked with the first couple of boys. Somehow word must have got out and suddenly more boys – and a few girls – wanted to fight me.

Ustath Nabil's suspicions were raised when he passed the park and noticed a big gang of children. They had formed a circle around Abdullah and me. Truth to tell, at that point I had lost it with Abdullah. He is the first Grade 5 boy I've fought and he is huge. Two heads taller.

Abdullah has me on the ground and is socking me. I am kicking like a helpless cockroach. The other children are yelling and shouting and cheering. They have paid money, so they are here to see a good fight.

Demanding an entrance fee had been Thaer's idea. 'And maybe next month when you are really good we'll introduce betting.' I was impressed by his suggestion, even though I didn't really know how betting was supposed to work. But I was sure Thaer would figure it out.

Suddenly the shouts and cheers around Abdullah and me stop, as if turned off by one quick flick of a switch. I hear lots of feet running across the dried-out earth of the park. And only then do I notice that Abdullah has stopped punching me. Naturally, I can't see anything since I am blindfolded.

Ustath Nabil is extremely angry. Not with me, but with Abdullah. He believes Abdullah has forced me to put the scarf across my eyes and then beat me up like an innocent victim. I try to intervene, to say that it was my idea, but it's no use. Ustath Nabil doesn't believe me, thinks I just want to protect the boys.

The fights have brought Thaer and me closer. We are running a business together – like grown-ups. In addition, we are earning well. Most of it we save. We have heard Mum and Dad talk about travelling to another country, maybe even taking a boat. Mum is against the idea. Says everything will calm down. 'And anyway we don't have enough money,' she says. So they are talking about the monster! Dad is aware of it after all! I am relieved that I am no longer alone. Yet at the same time I am upset that Mum doesn't want to seek help. Dad clearly thinks the monster problem is serious, otherwise he wouldn't suggest travelling.

In the early stages of our business all the money goes to Thaer. He says he's our business's accountant and an accountant looks after the money. I trust him – Thaer doesn't like spending – but then it strikes me that I could do with some cash so I can complete my preparations to fight the monster. Yet Thaer can't know why I need the money. I have never told him about the monster. So I ask for a salary. Everyone in a business receives a salary for their work. Thaer likes the idea very much, it sounds professional, he says.

It is around this time that I start to think I'll soon be ready to fight the monster, so I need to put together a strategy of how to attract the monster's attention. I want to talk to old Umm Kutub, she knows all about jinns and angels and devils and monsters – how to calm them and release them and control them, and also how to get rid of them for good. But I don't want to talk to her too soon. Just in case she goes running to my parents or my aunties and uncles.

The first two who stop coming to school from my class are Khalid and his twin sister, Batoul. They didn't tell anyone. Rumour soon spreads that they are now living in Canada and go to school there. The rest of us feel sorry for our friends, because we like the idea of travelling and going on holidays, but we all agree that we like to return home. That's the whole point of travelling, isn't it! To come back home. What a nice cosy feeling. One of the best feelings in the world. Everything looks a bit new, a bit different, a bit exciting, a bit changed. And yet, after a day or two, it feels as if I've never been away. My friends are still there and my road and even Umm Faisal, who is always so mean to us and complains when we play out on the street and chases us away, I'm somehow always a bit happy to see her when I come back after staying with my grandparents, or once when we went on holiday to Beirut.

Then more children go to live abroad, to Turkey, Lebanon, Egypt. Others go to stay with their grandparents and don't return. I hear Mum and Dad whisper more and more intensely every night about travelling. Dad tries to persuade Mum that we should go to Greece and says that he will get tickets and a bus can drive us to the sea and then we take a boat. But Mum says she doesn't want to go, she is scared because none of us can swim.

I buy the knife from the juice seller at the edge of the park. If you have enough money he gets you anything you want. Every baby, even Hamza, my little brother, already knows that. I tell him I want a proper Russian army knife in a sheath. The juice seller never asks any questions. He just counts the money, nods, smiles and gives me a thick, slimy, dark-purple *tout* juice for free. I don't like mulberry, it's far too sweet, but I don't want to upset him so I accept the gift. It makes me feel sick and I am worried that I might throw up.

I have bought Sellotape. I strap the knife to my belly underneath my vest before I get home.

Now all I have to do is go to Umm Kutub, then I will be ready to fight the monster.

9

CAMPS are often the only safe space for people who have had to flee from their country, who have had to turn their backs on homes and motherlands. It is our duty to ensure that these spaces continue to exist.

His voice is soft and his slight body rocks from side to side. He buries his hands deep in his trouser pockets. He gives off an aura of shyness and the shyness isn't put on. Yet he also lives for moments like these, when he knows that he has the audience's full attention. And now his voice begins to get stronger, his stature to grow. He is a magician. A poet. A truth-bearer. He has taken upon himself the hardship of travelling around the world for many weeks a year to draw attention to the injustices that his people are facing – still facing, years after the outbreak of the war. Through him their stories get heard. He is tirelessly, relentlessly fighting against the world's desire to forget the catastrophe it helped to create in the first place. He works towards a better future. Towards a society where everyone will be respected. Where everyone will have a place, a voice.

The international community and humanitarian aid organizations have already begun to collaborate with refugee camps to preserve their inhabitants' indigenous culture. These communities have taken displacement and flight – often at high personal risk – upon themselves so that their local identities and social knowledge will not be destroyed by Russian or American or British warplanes or hacked to pieces by Al-Qaida and ISIS.

It is thus our responsibility to help these refugees to preserve and safeguard their identity.

Tony opens his arms wide from behind his speaker's rostrum,

looking down into the packed auditorium. He always asks for a little stool that he can stand on behind the rostrum so that he appears taller. He imagines himself as an eagle, observing from above, seeing all, understanding all.

Do you believe in progress, in education, in development? Yes? But have you ever stopped to ask yourself the following question: what do these words mean in a world where over the last century and a half we have proved that these beliefs, these mantras lead only to the destruction of our planet? Just look at women's emancipation – and I am all for equality, this is just an example. Hasn't this development gone hand in hand with industrialization and the undoing of the very environment – the air, the forests, the oceans, the ice caps – that we humans require to live and to breathe?

We cannot turn back the clock. We should not stop educating our children and grandchildren. But we should be wary of imposing our philosophy on others.

Full house: three hundred people, the organizer said. Middle-aged couples looking for a cause. Young people looking for inspiration. Impressed that he escaped the war. Even though, of course, he didn't. He was miles away as the catastrophe was unfolding. He has lived abroad since his early teens. First he went to boarding school in the English countryside, then he studied in London and Paris. When the war broke out, he had been staying on a friend's sofa in the south of France for over a year already, trying to finish his first poetry collection.

Maybe we don't have the answer. But older cultures – like the cultures preserved in the villages where many of the refugees I am now serving come from – might have retained secrets, might have retained answers. And in these communities, the survival of the family and the clan has always been paramount, over and above the egoistic and self-centred needs of the individual.

Maybe progress as we understand it needs to be reconsidered.

At first Tony had been shocked to see what spilled over the borders of the land of his birth out into the world: tens of thousands, hundreds of thousands, millions of illiterate, uneducated, poor country people who might as well have come straight out of biblical – no, prehistoric – times. And each woman with at least two children in her arms and another on the back and number four in her belly, and she herself not much older than twenty but looking more like forty.

So how can we help to preserve these old cultures, help the refugees to hold on to their identity, their dignity inside the camps, even though from the outside these safe spaces look like breeding-grounds of ignorance, hopelessness and deprivation? How can we prevent the do-gooders in our world from going into refugee camps and destroying traditional cultures with Western-influenced colonial ideas and education?

The 'poet' adds colour and interest for the foreign audience – they certainly love that kind of shit. Yes, *shit*. He shouldn't have done it, ever, but then it was easy. He was invited to travel to Europe. He only needs to open his mouth and smile and say, 'I'm a Syrian poet,' and they think he escaped bombs and torture and Assad and prison and death, fleeing on foot across the border and then by boat, a little dinghy, across the Mediterranean, watching his mother die of hypothermia. He doesn't say any of this. But he sees in their eyes that this is what they see. What they want to see. Because they long for the gruesome bits – the bombs, the torture, the death – as well as the articulate part, the tame part, the part they can recognize, that speaks their language, beautiful, flawless English and French, because after all he is well educated, but with a touch of an accent, so he is still authentic. And it's easy for him to raise money, the charity is growing and it feels good, what he is doing. But it only feels good when he is travelling, being invited to London and Paris and New York and Sydney, attending conferences to talk about cultural identity and humanity.

What is a humane society? Surely it is one where everyone lives with dignity and is allowed their own cultural identity. Therefore, while it is of course important that humanitarian organizations offer awareness-raising courses for teenagers and adults in refugee camps on topics such as sex education and the dangers of early marriage, the participants should always get paid, ideally with food vouchers, but if that is not possible, in cash. In this way we will encourage the attendance of teenage girls and mothers, because if they generate an income it is in the interests of the family to send them. And moreover, the payment should be calculated in relation to the participant's immediate family size. Thus the more children a family has, the more they will earn, and we will be supporting and respecting the creation of big families rather than imposing Western, urban, nuclear-family ideals. In addition, it should also always be ensured that there are some educational facilities in the camps, especially for kindergarten and primary school children, as this is when most of the families are keen to educate their children. The financing and organization of these facilities, however, needs to be driven by national and international NGOs*, so that these institutions can be run as projects lasting a few months, at most one or two years. This will guarantee that if the projects are counterproductive or even hostile to the local cultures and identities of the refugees, they can be adjusted and refined within the next funding cycle, or, if considered necessary, stopped all together.*

10

THERE are many weeks when Mr Tony isn't in his apartment. But whenever he is there, he sits in the chair by the balcony door, reading and writing on his laptop. When Shams arrives, they might have a brief chat for a couple of minutes. Never longer. Yet she is sure that the more she sees him, the more he smiles at her. A couple of times he even laughs out loud. She puts him at ease, she thinks. She lightens the heavy burden on his thin shoulders. She loves making him laugh. She loves making him bestow his most beautiful gift on her: his smile.

And it is this smile that convinces Shams that Mr Tony is the most inspiring man she has ever met.

Before Mr Tony, no one had ever given her a book. Maybe as a child, back home, but she can't remember. She had read *The Trial*. It had taken her a couple of weeks. It was the first time she had read a novel. Little in the story made sense to her. She worried she hadn't had enough education to understand it. She wanted to talk to Mr Tony about the book. Why had he given it to her? What was she supposed to learn from it? She felt sorry for this man in the book, Joseph K. He didn't deserve to die. But there again, the story was so absurd. Maybe she hadn't understood. But when she next saw Mr Tony, he appeared preoccupied and simply said, 'You are a good pupil,' which made her feel proud, and then he gave her a new book, about the history of colonialism. Again she read it. Again she would have loved to talk to him about it. Again there was no time.

She reads all the books that he gives her. She knows he is trying to educate her. She worries that he will think she is not up to it. She feels stupid because she doesn't understand most of what is written in the books. Mr Tony is clearly encouraging her to seek knowledge. And so she spends her nights studying the books over and over again. And the more sleep-deprived she becomes, the more she is looking for hidden messages to soothe her aching heart. And the more intensely she searches, the more frequently she finds them. He is reaching out to her, even though he is aware that he shouldn't. After all, he is Christian, she is Muslim. And yet she senses that he is in torment as much as she is.

And then on one visit she notices that he is no longer wearing the chain with the little golden cross. 'Your cross,' she mumbles, without realizing that she has said the word out loud.

She sees Mr Tony's hand go up to where his cross used to be. For an instant his face shows confusion, bewilderment. Then it breaks out into the most beautiful smile she has yet seen. She has to close her eyes. It is so radiant, so light, so grateful, so happy. Tears well up inside her.

'My faith has been shaken,' she hears him say.

She opens her eyes again. 'I know, *habibi*, darling,' she wants to whisper. Yet this time the words don't cross her lips. She can't get herself to pronounce them. Instead, for a few seconds they silently look into each other's eyes.

This night she doesn't study the books. She sinks into a deep, dreamless sleep.

~

I have a dream in which all my school friends, including the ones who have already left, are standing by the roadside as the bus with my mum and my two brothers and me drives past. They are begging me to take them with us, offering me my favourite colours – white jasmine, bright-pink pickled turnip like in the shawarma, the orange *sabbara* cactus fruit. In the dream I am trying to figure out how to loosen the knife from my belly without my mother noticing. Then

I could lean out of the window and pick up the offerings with the knife's edge and that would make the bus stop.

~

Shams falls ever deeper in love with the mystery of Tony's being. In her head she now calls him Tony, no longer Mr Tony. She decides to read all the books on his shelves so that she will share his knowledge. She falls asleep with a book in her hand and the moment she wakes up she lifts it and continues reading. When she cooks, when she cleans, when she massages her aunt's feet, her eyes are glued to the page. Whenever Tony returns from his travels, she relishes the fleeting moments of his glorious smiles.

She imagines a fusing, a merging of minds, her female mind, his male mind, and it will be like the most glorious firework, and together they will create the just, dignified society for all humanity that he dreams about.

She becomes convinced that his thinking is more profound and deeper than she has ever imagined, and the longer she works for him, the less she expects him to share his complicated thoughts. How could she even have dared to dream of it? She has nothing to contribute, nothing to add. She attended school only to Grade 3, has never set foot in a secondary school, never written an essay.

It takes Shams two years, four months and twenty-one days to work through all the books in Tony's apartment. In the process she teaches herself English and French. She can't speak either language but reads them well now. Yet she is also aware that she doesn't understand every word. And even if she has previously encountered the words, their meaning eludes her. Perhaps that is why, when she has finished reading the four hundred and eight books (not, as Tony believed, thousands), she feels not that much wiser for it. She could put her knowledge in a nutshell: men are greedy and, given power, exploit it, and that's why a lot of absurdity happens in the world. Oh, and religions cause awful wars. And women? Their voices, at least on Tony's bookshelves, are completely absent. It is a dismal picture that Shams has gained of the world, much darker and more hopeless than the narrowest alleyways of the camp. In the camp there is at least always the chance of a stray ray of sunshine suddenly breaking through, or the innocent laughter of playing children, or a woman who has made herself beautiful for a lover. And even though this lover may not last, the woman is determined to grab her moment. Because in the camp there are these moments, and the possibility that one or other of them might lead to something unexpected.

Sitting at the table in Tony's apartment, in front of a simple walnut half filled with all the knowledge she has gained from reading a quarter of a million pages, disappointment brushes Shams's heart. Indeed, she now remembers that she felt the same disenchantment years ago when Tony gave her that first book and then never asked for her opinion. Has she lived an illusion?

Calmly she stands up and, for the first time in over three years, she decides to leave the apartment before she has finished cleaning. She needs to walk, to think, to breathe. And this time she will walk back to the camp and not take the taxi that Tony pays for.

She closes the shutters to the balcony door. As she turns round, her eyes fall on his laptop, which is beside where he sat in the morning when she arrived and where he left it when he hurried out of the apartment after receiving a phone call. For a moment she hesitates, then she opens it with a racing heart, her ears pricked in case the front door should open. She fully expects to close it straight away since she probably can't get any further without a password. Yet, to her surprise, the screen opens on a Word document. Her uncle's name, Abu Ali, catches her attention.

Here is a conversation that I recorded with one of the camp inhabitants, Abu Ali, fifty-five years old, on my recent research trip. Abu Ali is unemployed, illiterate, and has thirteen children by two wives. They live in two rooms. Abu Ali and I speak in our native tongue.

'A learning centre for children aged five to eleven is opening at the other side of the camp. Will you send your children?'

'What time do the lessons start?'

'Seven in the morning.'

'Too early, can't get them there in time.'

His wife whispers something into his ear. Abu Ali speaks.

'What's in it for us?'

'A food box and ten dollars per child per month.'

The wife speaks again with Abu Ali. Eventually he announces, 'We will send our children. But not every day.'

The second wife enters carrying a tray with tea glasses and a metal kettle. Abu Ali fills half my glass with sugar and then pours tea over it. I take a tiny sip, but still the sugar rush goes to my head. For a moment I close my eyes as my head is spinning. When I open them again, Abu Ali grins at me proudly.

'My woman makes good tea.'

I smile so as not to appear rude. Two young girls, who have until now lingered in a corner and observed me and my photographer from a safe distance, come closer. One hesitantly strokes my hair. I see this as a chance to ask another question that has been preying on my mind.

'Will you have more children?'

Without hesitation Abu Ali replies, 'Yes, of course. The young wife wants more children. I can't disappoint her.'

Education has taught us that the individual matters. That we have to respect each other. That we are all different.

Shams's legs are like jelly as she walks down the stairs, carefully sliding one foot in front of the other. She read his speech too, where he talked about cultural identity and education. Something is wrong. As she was reading a sour taste rose to her mouth. Now her throat feels dry, as if she hasn't drunk any water for days. It even crosses her mind that she might have been imprisoned for the last few years, abducted against her will. Outside the sun shines so brightly that it hurts her eyes, and the air is so humid that for a few moments she struggles to breathe. She begins walking down the road, first like an old woman, bent over, her feet skimming the ground. But with every step she also feels her muscles flexing back into action, longing to be used. Cultural identity doesn't mean ignorance, she suddenly thinks. Everyone needs education to function in the modern world, to understand the world, to be part of the world, to be able to have influence in the world. She feels anger rising inside her, her fighter's instinct awakening. And then suddenly something swooshes through the air. In a reflex reaction, she raises her arm and with a firm grip she prevents the attacker's next blow. When she realizes that her fist has closed in on itself, she stops mid-stride. She hasn't grasped anything between her fingers. There was no attacker. There *is* no attacker. Instead an insight struck her mind. So simple, yet powerful enough to nearly have thrown her off-balance. She should do something with her anger. Something useful. Her mother and her father were not ignorant people. Nevertheless they came from the same culture as her uncle, her aunt and many of the camp inhabitants. The difference: her parents believed in education. She feels someone - or something - or maybe just a breath of air - putting an arm around her, placing a soft kiss on her temple. *So Shams, what are you going to do with this insight?* whispers a soft voice.

Shams doesn't move. Shams doesn't breathe.

Then movement returns. She starts rummaging in her bag for her mobile phone. She pulls it out and scrolls down the list of contacts. She is now looking for the name and number of a Lebanese woman she met a while back when she was attending yet another awareness course in the hope that she might learn something new. That particular course had been run by an organization working against gender-based violence. At the end, the facilitator had pulled her aside.

Shams has reached 'R' in her contacts. *Roula*. That was her name. Roula was the facilitator.

'You should be teaching these courses,' Roula had said to Shams, 'not me. You are smart. You understand. And you come from the same background as the other young women. You live here. They will listen to you. They will never listen to me.'

Back then, Shams had stored Roula's number out of politeness, having no desire to teach any courses in the camp. Back then, all she was thinking about was how much she wanted to leave the camp.

'Hi Roula. This is Shams. Do you remember me? I'm wondering if I should open a learning centre for teenage girls in the camp. Can we meet?'

Shams will teach girls, girls from her own culture, to read and write and do maths and say no to early marriage and no to being second wives and no to having too many children. She will give herself and other girls a voice through education, through sustainable education. And then they will show the world that they are capable of far more than breeding endless children. She will put female refugee voices on Tony's bookshelf!

11

ENVY has glowing red eyes, wicked green hair and an ugly naked body. She jumps on you and buries her fangs in your neck and sucks the blood out of you. Once upon a time, you too ventured up onto the rooftop and pulled down the sun, drinking in its warmth and filling yourself up with its sparkling light. You began to stir and create something that shimmered just like you. And that is what envy can't tolerate. So she comes and sucks the blood out of you and you sink back to the bottom of the darkest alleyways where no sunlight ever penetrates. Where the smell of sewage is so strong you bend over and vomit, vomit for days until you think you are about to die. And then you curl up and rest your cheek on dry earth, and it feels like heaven. And you fall back into a blissful sleep, spending most of your days sleeping. You make sure you never attract envy's attention again. Because even the thought of being knocked back down another time is too painful to bear.

12

SHE doesn't mind the alleyways in the early hours of the morning when the camp is quiet, and the morning sun softens its edges, and the dirt and poverty and lack of space have a romantic, almost innocent look that promises a better day. But she only really comes alive later on, around eleven or twelve, when everyone starts waking up with a full bladder and grumbling bowels. Salt water is the only water coming out of the taps in the camp but it dries the skin and makes it itch, so many people don't wash, and many also sleep in the same clothes they wear during the day because the lack of privacy when sharing a single room with an extended family of ten or more makes changing clothes a complicated, tiresome operation. For Shatila, this is when the foul odours start to creep under her skin and pump up her veins and fill her alleyways with the stench of sweat from tens of thousands of bodies that haven't washed for weeks and the smell of the rubbish spilling out from the plastic bags that are dumped outside buildings in the evening, only to be torn apart at night by rats and cats, both of which fuse with the stink from the overflowing sewers that were originally intended for three thousand people and now have to deal with the excrement of over forty thousand. It is now that Shatila is happy.

PART THREE

13

THE image shows a girl in her late teens lying on a table, naked, belly down, her arms and legs spread wide, each held down by a man, with a fifth man standing between her legs inserting two bottles, one in her anus and one in her vagina.

The thumb of the hand that holds the mobile phone touches the screen. The image begins to move. Men cheering. A woman's high-pitch scream. Loud laughter.

Shams feels her heart missing a beat and bile rising up her throat and into her mouth. She turns her head away, swallowing the sour liquid down again. Then she walks to the other side of the room in order to be as far away as possible from the awful video.

The men are still cheering.

'Turn it off.'

It's Afifa. Shams recognizes her instantly. Her second cousin, with whom she used to spend a lot of time when they were young. Only a few days ago, Umm Ali mentioned that Afifa had got married and was now living in England.

14

WHEN I set up the charity, I never thought it would come to this. I was a poet wanting to help refugees, my compatriots. I never thought of myself. I was so naive. Yet what did I know? Now many people are dependent on me: my mother, my wife, my child. My cousins, who have all fled Syria. They all came to me, looking for employment. I couldn't let them down. Cousin Pierre is now our operations manager. My cousin Raja our comms person. And then there are old kindergarten friends, such as Louis. All of them, like me, have families to feed, bills to pay. They have no other opportunities.

15

AFIFA had stopped coming to Shams's centre a couple of months ago. Her mother said she had got engaged and was no longer interested in continuing her studies.

Shams had been so upset about Afifa leaving. She felt she had personally failed to make her cousin see that no one would help her unless she helped herself first through learning as much as she could and keeping her options open by not getting married. Afifa was smart and eager. Shams had always thought that Afifa wouldn't fall for marriage after all, and secretly she'd already dreamed of employing her in a couple of years' time as a teacher.

Afifa was among the first group of girls Shams had begun teaching, two years ago. She started with fifteen girls, most of them first or second cousins once or twice removed, since their mothers trusted Umm Ali and therefore Shams. Shams's reputation soon spread because she succeeded in getting the girls to read and write and do maths, and even market traders began to take notice as they could no longer cheat the families. One of the liveliest girls, Afifa was instrumental in spreading the reputation of the centre in the camp and bringing more girls to Shams. Now the centre has fifty girls who attend lessons four hours a day and it employs three full-time teachers. Shams is supported by the organization Roula is working for and has attracted the attention of two other funding organizations. She is hoping to expand her centre soon.

The secret of Shams's success is to be able to offer her fellow refugees what no one else offers: stability and continuity. As she tells everyone, her centre is here to stay. And even though the funders believe that each of them is supporting a separate fixed-term project,

Shams has designed things in such a way that these projects together form the backbone of a proper school. In addition she pays not a single lira or cent to the families of her students. Education is not a commodity sold by the families, but a right provided to the girls.

16

IN the beginning, I used to feel very uneasy whenever someone at a conference or talk indirectly or even directly suggested that I too am a refugee, a displaced person who cannot go back to their home country. I'm a poet, I thought, a free spirit. I have always lived in different countries, never felt the desire to return to my birth country except for summer holidays.

17

'Do you know the girl?' Tony now asks.

He has stopped the video and slides the mobile phone back into his pocket. Shams nods.

It is the first time in two years that he has come to see her in her centre in Shatila, despite the fact that he has of course been aware of it from the beginning. For the first six months after Shams discovered Tony's speeches, she had continued working for him as a cleaner. She never confronted him about what she had read on his laptop, though. But back then she asked him to double her fee as a cleaner – and pay in dollars. This extra money helped her to start the education centre.

There was something about Tony's visit that had made her tense even before he showed her the video. With a sense of foreboding, a nerve twisted in her lower back and pain shot up her neck the moment she saw him standing at the door as she was coming up the stairs to unlock the centre for the teachers and girls.

'Was she one of your students?' Tony continues.

For a moment Shams hesitates before answering. A thick cloud of suspicion hangs in the air. Why? From where? She wipes the cloud away, replying in the affirmative.

Then she asks him, 'Who sent you this video?'

18

MOTHERS in the camp receive lucrative offers from abroad to marry their daughters. But Afifa's mother, Umm Khalid, had initially said no. Then she changed her mind. After all, it was her cousin Umm Ali, Shams's aunt, who had brought the suitor to their doorstep.

Umm Ali introduced Umm Khalid to a distant cousin on her husband's side, a respectable, pious man who had come unexpectedly from Saudi to visit. Umm Ali had never met this man before but Abu Ali invited him in for tea and they talked deep into the night about their village before the war. This distant cousin told them that his nephew, a good, trustworthy boy called Hassan, had fallen in love with Umm Khalid's eldest daughter, Afifa. Hassan had seen the girl's photo on Facebook and had begun enquiring who she might be and if she was already married. He asked everyone, as he was so in love with this girl he couldn't stop thinking about and was desperate to find out if she was already taken. When he discovered that she was still available and even from the same clan his heart rejoiced.

At first Umm Khalid didn't want to mention anything to her daughter about this young Saudi man called Hassan. Umm Khalid had heard about groups who groom young refugee women from the camps and then sell them as sex slaves worldwide. So she was afraid for the safety of her daughter. But then this young man, who was after all the nephew of her cousin's husband, rang her up on FaceTime. He was dressed nicely and sat in an expensive apartment, so Umm Khalid let him speak to Afifa, but not without cautioning him.

'Young man, my daughter is getting an education. She will not yet marry.'

Soon Afifa and Hassan were talking every day. He was helping her with her English and maths homework. Afifa, of course, didn't mention in the centre why she had suddenly got even better at her studies. She knew that Shams would disapprove.

One day Umm Khalid remembered her initial fear about the sex slave trade. She laughed at herself. Surely, no one who is only interested in slaves spends hours helping a stupid girl with her homework.

She could see that Afifa liked Hassan more and more because she now spent long hours in front of the mirror before each FaceTime video call.

Then one day Afifa showed her mother a photo of a letter that Hassan had sent her on WhatsApp. Afifa explained that this letter was from a school in Jeddah offering her a place as a mature student. Umm Khalid couldn't read but Afifa read the letter to her. And it had a big stamp on it.

'Please, Mum, let me marry him,' Afifa begged. 'He cares about my education and he will show me the world.'

Like every girl in the camp, Afifa dreamed of a prince or an *Ibn Halal*, a Son of Decency, a handsome young man who would change her life and allow her to become what she wanted to be: loved and successful. And even though she had heard Shams say many times that unless a girl learned to find self-esteem and ambition and success inside herself, no one would be able to fill that gap, Afifa was now convinced that she had found an exception with Hassan. The world would soon see how successful she'd be at her Jeddah school and eventually she'd become a famous doctor.

Moreover, Hassan was also offering five thousand dollars as bride money. And he had already sent the first five hundred dollars via Western Union, Umm Khalid could pick it up whenever she wanted. And so Umm Khalid and Abu Khalid were satisfied that this young man obviously valued their daughter.

The marriage was arranged and held over Zoom. A passport was organized for Afifa and she flew to Dubai, where they were going to spend their honeymoon. Five days went by and Umm Khalid didn't hear from her daughter. But she wasn't worried. Hassan had explained to her, 'You might not hear straight away from your daughter. I booked a wedding suite on the top of the world to introduce her to the dream world that she will be living in from now on.'

However, when an entire week passed without news from Afifa, Umm Khalid did start to worry. But whenever she tried Hassan's or Afifa's phone, it was always switched off. She went to Umm Ali and asked her to speak to her husband's cousin. Abu Ali called his distant cousin, who reassured him that all was fine. The happy couple hadn't yet arrived in Jeddah, they were extending their honeymoon in Dubai. They didn't want to be disturbed.

Another two weeks passed.

By now surely they must have arrived in Jeddah, Umm Khalid thought, waking up in a cold sweat. Afifa's new school had started and she had been so excited about it.

'A proper school. A private school, Mum. When I graduate from there, I can go to any university I want to.'

Afifa would never have missed the first day.

Again, Umm Khalid went to Umm Ali. The young couple still hadn't arrived in Jeddah, but the cousin reassured the women that he had spoken to Hassan only two days previously. The young couple were now in London. Afterwards they might go to Paris. They had decided to explore the world together.

'But what about Afifa's studies?' Umm Khalid's voice was shrill, shaking as she cut into the conversation.

There was a moment's silence before the line went dead.

'Call him back,' Umm Khalid shrieked. The panic that had lingered in her intestines for days had suddenly risen to her throat and was tightening its grip.

At the other end, the phone was turned off.

'How well . . . did you . . . know this . . . cousin before . . .

he arrived?' Umm Khalid had to pause every two words, her breath had become that short.

Umm Ali bent closer over the phone, pressing the little receiver icon again and again.

'Cousin Fatimah from Idlib called Abu Ali and said that Cousin Abdullah from Jeddah was coming to Beirut and wanted to see us. So of course I couldn't say no,' she whispered eventually.

Umm Khalid took Umm Ali by the shoulders and began shaking her.

'Why didn't you say to her: "But who is this Cousin Abdullah, I don't know him?" Why didn't you, why didn't you?'

Tears were streaming down her cheeks. Umm Khalid knew that she wouldn't get an answer from Umm Ali. There was no answer. When relatives come and knock on your door you cannot deny them entry. That would be rude, unacceptable behaviour.

Umm Khalid went home, lay down on the mattress with her face to the wall and decided to die. She feared the worst.

That evening she received a call from a withheld number. Afifa's voice came from far away.

'Mum!' It sounded like a cry for help, as if she was trying not to weep. But then she said, 'I'm fine. Everything is fine. I'm in London, you know, in England, with the king.'

'And how is Hassan?'

'Hassan?' Afifa's voice sounded confused. Or maybe Umm Khalid imagined it. There was a lot of noise in the background and someone was talking to her daughter. 'Yes, Hassan is fine too. We are very happy. I have to go now, Mum. Bye.'

And the line went dead.

For about ten minutes Umm Khalid sat motionless with the phone in her lap. Inside her head a big dark abyss had opened up and she was staring down into it. She hardly breathed: there were no thoughts, no feelings, no way forward, no way backwards. She was waiting. And maybe this waiting would continue forever. Then her brain latched on to the words: 'I'm fine. Everything is fine. We are in London, you know, in England, with the king.'

Yes, Afifa was fine. She said it herself. There was no more need for doubt. And Umm Khalid went to Umm Ali and told her the good news.

And it isn't until Mr Tony knocks on Umm Khalid's door and shows her the video that she breaks down in violent sobs and can no longer keep reality at bay. Mr Tony tells her that Afifa isn't the only one, there is at least one other girl from the camp they know of. He will get them out, Mr Tony promises. And they know who is responsible for all of this.

'Who?'

Mr Tony goes to the other end of the room and sits down on the mattress. He deeply empathizes with the woman's plight – the world is such a cruel place. But her smell, a mixture of old woman's sweat, pee and rancid cooking fat, makes the hairs on his neck stand up and he has to suppress a retch. He now watches her as she drops to her knees and crawls on all fours towards him, sobbing.

'Who? Who? Please tell me who can do such a horrible thing to my daughter. Please help me, please help me.'

Umm Khalid falls flat on her stomach and takes his socked feet between her hands and begins kissing them.

Mr Tony is petrified. He stops breathing. This is too much for him and he wants to leave.

He closes his eyes to gather all his strength and willpower and swallow the bile that has come up into his mouth involuntarily when he realizes how many germs this woman might right now be spreading on his feet.

Bending forward, he places his hand benevolently on the top of her headscarf.

'Please sit down and I will tell you.'

She buries her nose between his feet and presses them together and sobs for a little while longer. Finally, she crawls back to her place on the mattress at the other side of the room, takes a paper tissue out of the box and blows her nose.

Mr Tony says, 'Shams.'

19

CAMILLE – the apple of my eye, my saviour, my support, the strongest woman I have ever known – came to me at a time when I had lost all hope of ever finding true love. On my lonely travels I had begun to frequent dating sites. A few times I arranged to meet a woman. I always organized the meetings in such a way that it was on the last night that I spent in a certain hotel and city, so that there would be no danger of bumping into her again in case the evening didn't go well and we didn't want to see each other again. I was aware I was awkward around women. And how could I not be? I had no experience.

I never saw a woman twice and I never let anyone stay the night in a hotel room with me. That is until I met Camille. For a year, wherever I gave a lecture, she was there, sitting in the front row, always asking the first audience question. At the beginning I wasn't sure if I had seen this woman before. She never came up to me afterwards, while a lot of other people did. Eventually I was sure it was the same woman. Initially I panicked. Was she a spy? A secret agent? Why did she never approach me outside the lecture halls? Then one day I saw her sitting in my hotel lobby. Without thinking I went straight up to her. She was reading a book and didn't see me coming. I wanted to say something unfriendly. My eyes fell on the book. It was the Bible. Suddenly all the aggression and fear went out of my body. I smiled at her. She smiled at me. For the following weeks we talked for hours on WhatsApp. When I knew I'd be going to Europe again soon, I asked her to marry me. She said yes. The next time, only the second time we saw each other face to face, we went to a register office in Paris, Camille's home town.

Camille and I agreed that she would remain living in Paris and I would bring my mother, who had been staying with her sister in Amman since 2011, to live with her. At the same time, I would continue working in Lebanon, running the charity. Since Camille is as passionate as I am about the cause, we decided after the birth of our daughter that she too would work for our organization. This gives us more income. Camille is now head of monitoring and evaluation.

My relatives and old friends of course know that I'm married. But otherwise I haven't made a public announcement. I like to keep my two lives separate.

20

YOU know what it means when rumours begin circulating ever faster in the camp, like thick slime running along the paths and alleyways, mingling with the overflowing gullies and overloaded, broken sewage pipes, creating a dangerous toxic brew that leads to stomach cramps and often, with the old and the very young, death.

21

UMM Ali had been the first person to receive the video. The message came through from an unknown number on WhatsApp at 1 a.m. She wasn't asleep yet and felt the vibration underneath her abaya, which she always uses as a pillow. She pulled out the phone, brought it close to her face and without thinking pressed on the video that had been sent to her. It took her a couple of moments to figure out what was happening. She pressed the stop button. This was disgusting. Luckily her phone was on silent. She was about to delete the video when curiosity got the better of her. There was something that appeared familiar, even though she couldn't put her finger on it. She went to the kitchen and pressed 'play' again.

She had difficulty breathing. She drank a couple of glasses of water, constantly listening in case anyone had woken up. Had they too received the video? No one stirred. She held the phone in her sweaty hands, starring at it, waiting for Umm Khalid to ring her. Surely Umm Khalid must have been sent the same video? Otherwise it wouldn't make sense. Why her, Umm Ali, and not Umm Khalid? Surely if the sender had her number, they would also have Umm Khalid's number. After all, Umm Khalid was Afifa's mother.

For an hour, a painfully long hour, Umm Ali starred at her screen. But nothing.

She had to tell someone. She couldn't just sit here and keep it all in. The girl needed help.

For a fleeting moment she thought of waking up Shams. Shams had become such a leading figure in the camp with her girls' school.

And she knew everyone now, surely she would be able to get help. But something didn't feel right to Umm Ali about sharing this awful news with her niece and asking for her advice.

Of course, later, Umm Ali would know why her instinct had told her not to wake up Shams. And thank God she trusted her instinct.

Mr Tony came to Umm Ali's mind. Over the years he had been so good to them and so kind to Shams, employing her as a cleaner and never bearing a grudge when she decided to open her own centre. At the beginning he had even offered Shams the opportunity to teach for his organization but the silly girl had refused. Greedy as she was, she wanted her own thing. Yes, Mr Tony was the right person to talk to. He had people like Umm Ali's interests at heart, he would know what to do.

22

FOR a few moments Tony had stared utterly horrified at the video. Horror at what he saw, yes, but even more so at the ramifications. Afifa, he was sure, was registered with his charity. She had done a few courses with them some years ago. If this video was linked in any way to his organization, he would be forced to shut up shop. And he would lose everything.

23

ABOUT a year ago I tried to get a job in Paris, not least because flying back and forth is very expensive and during the first months of Covid there were long periods when I couldn't get to France at all. Naively, I assumed, given my experience working in Lebanon and the success of my international lectures, I would walk relatively quickly into a well-paid job with a European or Western organization. Yet I wasn't even invited for interviews.

'It's because you are a refugee,' my wife said.

'I'm not a refugee.' I was appalled by her suggestion.

'You are, darling. And there is nothing to be ashamed of. You are not like the refugees in the camps, but you are still a refugee. And that's why no one wants you.'

I thought about her words. And it was the next time I returned from Beirut, when I was stopped at Charles de Gaulle airport and interrogated for over an hour, despite the fact that I now have French residency, that I began to realize how I had internalized how the rest of the world saw me without ever questioning it. What was I doing in France? they were asking. Why had I married a French woman? Where had I met her? What had I been doing in Syria before the war? Why was I now working with Syrian refugees in Lebanon? It wasn't the first time that I had been exposed to such unsettling, suspicious questioning. But while before I just took it as an irritation and put it out of my mind as soon as I was waved through immigration, this time I permitted myself to feel the full impact of the degradation and humiliation. Indeed, I was treated as if I had no right to live a normal life and travel freely to see my wife and child and help my compatriots back in the camps. And it suddenly struck me that my wife was right: to them I was nothing but a stateless refugee who was not wanted in their country.

That night Camille woke me up because in my dream I had been crying.

24

Mr Tony rang Umm Ali immediately.

'Who sent you this video?'

'I don't know . . . I don't know.'

Umm Ali tried to swallow her tears but it was difficult. She felt somehow guilty, even though it wasn't her fault. It really wasn't her fault – she had already repeated it to herself a thousand times.

'Have you shown the video to anyone else? Sent it to anyone else?'

'No!'

'Has anyone else received it?'

'I don't know . . . I don't think so. Umm Khalid would have called me.'

'Who is Umm Khalid?' Tony snapped.

He had little patience talking to people like Umm Ali, who always assumed that you were familiar with all the minor details of their lives. They were utterly incapable of putting themselves in other people's shoes. Tony had of course forgotten that Umm Ali had mentioned her friend Umm Khalid before, many years ago, when Mr Tony was new in the camp. But Umm Ali hadn't forgotten.

'Afifa's mother.'

'And why would she have called you?'

'Because . . . because . . . I'm her cousin. We are friends.'

'Don't do anything until I call you again.'

It was pure luck that he was in Beirut and not in Paris. Tony jumped out of bed and got dressed even though it had only just gone three in the morning. He wouldn't be able to go back to sleep and needed to be at Shams's centre as soon as it opened.

Umm Ali was Shams's aunt and, as he had just learned, she was also related to Umm Khalid, Afifa's mother. For a split second, Tony was puzzled. Why would anyone be sending the link to Umm Ali and not to Umm Khalid? Unless . . . of course . . . the sender was trying to point the finger at . . . Shams, who was the common link between Umm Ali, Umm Khalid and Afifa.

Over the next few hours, as Tony watched the small hand of his watch creep painfully slowly forward, he persuaded himself more and more that Shams might be the source of all evil. At the same time, he was aware that Shams's guilt in the matter suited him, as it would decrease the possibility of anyone suspecting his organization being involved in this horrendous crime. Therefore, until he spoke to Shams, he decided to try very hard to keep an open mind, to not accuse her without proof. He liked the girl. For a refugee she had shown impressive initiative. This centre of hers was growing and its reputation was spreading. Still, Tony suddenly began to see how she had probably made the money that allowed her to employ teachers and expand her centre so rapidly.

And there was another thing. Already while Shams was working for him, Tony had noticed an arrogance within her. Just because she enjoyed reading and learning, that shouldn't have allowed her to feel superior to the other girls and women in the camp. But it did. How would she otherwise have plucked up the courage to start her own project? There were many voices who praised Shams, impressed by her desire to do good for her community rather than wanting to leave the camp as quickly as possible. But it never made sense to him. Refugees living inside a camp always only think about getting out. Everyone would, wouldn't they? For someone to suddenly say that they actually want to stay and, moreover, to have a sustainable impact, that just wasn't logical. Unless, of course, they weren't thinking about their community at all. In an instant the picture became clear to him. Shams was only thinking about herself, using her little project to enrich herself and, probably, arrogantly and criminally exploiting the other girls and young women to that end.

Still, until he spoke to her, Tony would not give up hope.

25

I have now accepted the fact that I too am a refugee. The only thing that separates me from my compatriots living in the camps is my job. If the organization folds and I lose my job, I will have nothing.

26

'I will get my girl back. This woman is the devil personified. She is laughing at all of us. Thinks because I can't read that I can't fight for my daughter.'

Umm Khalid is speaking straight into the camera. She is so agitated, spit comes out of her mouth and dribbles down her chin. For a second the camera lingers on her face. Then it sways to the person standing next to her.

'It is my duty as a compatriot, a fellow exile, to help this poor woman get her daughter back. And people like Shams have to be stopped.'

The camera moves to Umm Khalid again.

'How much are you suing Shams for?'

Umm Khalid throws a quick sidelong glance at Mr Tony before she answers: 'One . . . one hundred dollars.'

'One hundred thousand dollars,' Tony whispers between clenched teeth, while trying to move his lips as little as possible.

'One hundred thousand dollars,' Umm Khalid repeats.

27

SHAMS had been punished enough. You have to believe me, I didn't want her to suffer more. After the scandal broke, her centre had to close down. And it will remain closed forever. After all, what kind of mother or father would still allow their daughter to attend such a place of mistrust. Moreover, Shams hasn't been seen at all since her crime became public knowledge. I also feel sorry for Abu Ali and Umm Ali. They are good people, and raised their niece as best they could after her family vanished. They don't deserve all this agony.

28

It's time to prepare myself. I pull the knife out of its sheath. I feel the blade. It's super sharp. I place it beside me. Then I take off my T-shirt. I'd love to tear it, it'd be easier to use as a blindfold. But I no longer want to make any unnecessary noise. Just in case the monster is already in the room. I blindfold myself. At the moment it doesn't make any difference, but I want to eliminate any risk. I'm a better fighter in pitch-darkness. What if the monster doesn't come until dawn is already breaking, though?

I sit quietly. Hardly breathe. I can't hear my mum. I shuffle over to her. Put my ear to her mouth. Her breathing is very shallow, very weak. I crawl back into my corner. Perhaps the monster is already here. My hand closes around the knife.

My head jerks back. Did I fall asleep? I can't feel the knife in my hand. A strange, dangerous noise overhead. A high-pitched sh-shing sound.

The monster. I'm ready. I want to jump to my feet.

Then—

A deafening bang like an explosion. My back against the wall. Shaking all around me.

Something very heavy on top of me.

Nothing.

29

I know how the rumour mill works in the camp. People can suddenly turn against anyone. Even if proved innocent. One has to be prepared. You all of course know by now that my organization has nothing to do with the abduction cases. But that doesn't protect me or my organization. I can't afford camp opinion suddenly turning against us, with the possibility of losing donors, of having to shut our doors. My family's survival depends on the organization.

I knew that if Umm Khalid sued Shams, making a public statement, it would leave no doubt whatsoever who the culprit was. Even the rumour mill couldn't then churn out another story. The idea, however, was never that Umm Khalid should *really* sue Shams. I didn't want that to happen. Umm Khalid just needed to believe that she wanted to sue Shams and say it out loud. So I organized a camera team from one of the Facebook camp news channels to record the statement and put it on their feed. No one except people living inside the camp watch these channels anyway. But Umm Khalid of course didn't know that.

Abu Ali and Umm Ali would be shown the clip, I was sure. And I was also convinced that they would offer Umm Khalid money to take it no further. They wouldn't want it to go to court, they would want to keep it in the family.

30

WHEN Omar knocks on their door and asks for Shams's hand, Abu Ali's instinctive reaction is to scold the young man for being unkind, for making such a bad joke. Only Omar's reputation prevents Abu Ali from doing so. Omar has been back in the camp for well over a year now. He arrived from Norway with a long beard, wearing long white robes and feeling disappointed and let down by the West. Within two months he had married a fifteen-year-old girl, and now has a son and a second child on the way. He gives lectures to teenage boys who are preparing to join ISIS in Syria about the end of the world and the holy war and life in paradise.

In short, Omar is not the type to make jokes. Abu Ali knows that. So he invites Omar in and offers him tea, and Omar says that as a dowry he will settle the dispute with Umm Khalid.

This brings tears to Abu Ali's eyes. A huge burden is lifted from his shoulders. And there and then the two men agree on the marriage.

In the night Shams tries to run away. She knows where there are women's shelters in Beirut. She should have run away when all this madness started. Yet she was convinced that people would eventually speak up. They know she has nothing to do with what's happening to Afifa and the other girl. Especially her aunt and Umm Khalid know. They know her. But they don't dare stand up to Shatila's rumour mill. In case it turns against them.

Shams waits till everyone is asleep, then she quietly gets up. The front door is locked.

'I have the key here with me,' she hears her aunt's voice in the dark. 'You will marry Omar tomorrow, and he will settle up with Abu Khalid and everything will return to normal.'

'I won't,' Shams says, defiance in her voice.

31

HER uncle and cousins are prepared. They have sticks at the ready. Shams's screams resound through the alleyways. It was to be expected. After all, the woman has gone too far.

32

HER head is inside a wooden box. She can't turn it to the right or the left. She can't move it at all. She can only scream. And she realizes that the box is stuck between two walls. It is holding her in so tightly that she can take her feet off the ground and wiggle her entire body from her neck down. But that's all she can do: wiggle her body. Her head, her thoughts, her imagination remain stuck, utterly stuck. Where is she?

She's been imprisoned. And no sound can get out.

33

'I will protect you,' Omar whispers. 'You are mine now forever. I will never let you go again.'

34

HE came to her centre straight after returning from Norway. He said he was getting an apartment ready in the camp. As soon as that was done they could get married. Shams had looked at Omar in amazement. They hadn't spoken for years. She had simply shaken her head.

'I like you as a friend. But I can't marry you.'

She realized he hadn't expected such a reaction.

'You are mine. You gave yourself to me.'

'I was young then.'

He had turned on his heels without saying goodbye.

PART FOUR

35

NO! Shams opens her mouth wide, gasping for air, the 'no' reverberating inside her head. She might have screamed out loud or just silently, she doesn't know. The scream fills her from the inside like a balloon and she shoots up from the depths of the ocean where she was lying, holding her breath for a very long time. Vegetating, surviving.

Period blood is running out of her. She smells it before she can feel it. She brings her hand between her legs, then lifts her red fingertips to her eyes, to be sure. She rubs her fingers against each other, smelling the blood, inhaling it. She licks the blood off her fingertips. The taste of iron sinks into her like an anchor.

She is lying on a mattress, on her side, facing the wall. She has lain here since they brought her, maybe a month ago, maybe longer. She wonders if it is the first time that she's had her period since she was forced to marry Omar. She can't remember. She has faced the wall most of the time. Nour, Omar's first wife, brings her food. Shams remembers seeing spoons appearing in front of her face and opening her mouth obediently. At night Omar would come and she'd feel his hand on her shoulder. He'd turn her around onto her back, do what he thought a husband has the right to do. She didn't care.

Shams doesn't know where this 'no' has come from. But now it is here, it fills her out. She sits up and leans her back against the wall. There is a glass of water by her mattress. She takes it and drinks. The room is tiny and square. There is a door at one end, standing ajar, light stealing in. No windows. The air is hot and humid. A fan is fixed to the ceiling in the corner to her left. It isn't working even though it is plugged in and the dial points to three. The electricity must have cut out. There is a blue plastic mat with yellow flowers on the floor. Along the wall opposite a small child is asleep, naked, just wearing nappies. Shams's outstretched legs nearly touch its mattress. That's how small the room is. In fact, it is not a room, it is more like a cell.

I can't get pregnant. The thought appears clearly in her mind now. She senses that over the previous weeks she'd been searching for such a tangible, clear goal and had struggled to find it. But now, with the onset of her period, she understands what she needs to do. She has to get hold of the pill. She will ring Roula. Roula will be able to help her.

Nour is sitting on the floor in the small kitchen stuffing courgettes. Shams steps over the plastic bowl with the bulgur mixture. Blood is running down the inside of her leg.

'He will not be pleased,' Nour says without any intonation, her hands continuing to stuff the vegetables.

Shams must have stepped over her sister-wife's bowls many times before on her way to the bathroom, but she can't remember.

She continues on her way to the toilet without responding. Nour may be her friend or her foe. She doesn't know. Perhaps if Shams stretched out her hand to this tiny sixteen-year-old girl who looks more like twelve – her belly round for the second time, as she's now seven months pregnant – she would take it and Shams could make an ally of her.

But sister-wives are not meant to be each other's best friends. They are set up to compete for a man's attention and love.

'Can I borrow your phone?' Shams asks Nour when she comes back into the kitchen, guessing the answer before she receives it but wanting to be sure.

'Omar has the phone. He will be back in a couple of hours.'

Shams goes back to her mattress and turns once again to the wall. But this time she stays on the surface, wide awake. She wants to live. She wants Shatila to acknowledge her innocence. She wants to open her centre again.

She could of course walk out of the door, and out of the camp, to one of the women's shelters. No one would stop her, unless she was unlucky and bumped into Omar. Even if she met her uncles or cousins, they wouldn't stop her. They would probably look away, pretending they hadn't seen her. She is Omar's property, Omar's responsibility now. No longer theirs.

But if she were to walk out looking for refuge elsewhere, she could never return.

36

IT takes Shams two full days to realize that if she can just walk out of the camp intending never to return without anyone stopping her, she can equally easily walk out, see Roula to get the pill, and then return. Omar is the only person she has to make sure to avoid until she returns.

She gets up and gets dressed, pulling a black abaya that she finds hanging on the door over her clothes and drawing the black hijab well over her face.

The front door is locked.

'Give me the key,' Shams says to Nour.

'We are not allowed out, he has the key,' Nour replies.

Shams doesn't even think to stop. It is as if her subconscious has planned everything in advance without her being fully aware. She climbs over the wall of the small balcony that leads off the second room, the front room with the television. She jumps onto a roof covered in layers and layers of rubbish that she wades through, then hops down again a couple of metres and stands in a narrow alleyway. She turns left and walks to the corner, where she stops for a second and lifts her gaze to orientate herself. Luckily she knows straight away where she is. There are small shops – coffee shops and mobile phone shops and greengrocers – along the dried-mud path. She keeps on walking without looking up.

Later on, she will lie to Omar, telling him she's been to see a doctor. 'I suffered a miscarriage,' she will say. The doctor has informed her, she will claim, that if Omar wants them to have children, he can only have sex with her twice a week. She will have debated the number with herself on the way back from seeing Roula. Shams doesn't want to have sex with Omar at all. Yet if Omar is to buy into her game, she can't undermine his dignity, she has to respect his manhood – or what she knows he considers his manhood to be: his right and duty to have sex with his wives. She would have been tempted to say only once a week – but she is sure Omar would not accept that. Twice sounds more realistic, as if there is indeed a doctor's concern for their procreative obligation behind that decision.

And she needs Omar to believe in the story so that he will cooperate, certain that Shams has now accepted their marriage and her duties towards her husband. This in turn will make it possible for Shams to move freely again in the camp, to rebuild bridges with the mothers of her former pupils.

37

OMAR is lying on the floor, face down. Shams is sitting astride his lower back, bending his arms backwards.

'Tie his legs,' she orders Nour, who is standing somewhere in the corner behind her, shrieking. Omar is still in agony, but it is only a matter of moments before he will begin trying to free himself.

When Shams returned, he opened the door, pulled her in and began hitting her straight away. She was ready and intercepted his arms and kicked him hard between the legs. He doubled over and Shams brought both hands clenched into a fist down on the top of his back. He fell forward.

'If you do that—' he begins between clenched teeth, addressing himself to Nour.

Shams pushes herself forward, along his back and then presses her knees into the curve of his neck.

'Shut up!' she hisses.

Then she shouts, 'Nour, you stupid bitch, get a move on. Otherwise you are next.'

Nour ties Omar's legs with a scarf and Shams ties his hands with her hijab. Yet even after he is tied up, she remains seated on top of him. She wants him to hold still.

'My womb is weak.' She is now making it up as she goes along. 'This is why too much sex can easily lead to miscarriages. I also need a phone,' she adds, while keeping up the pressure on his neck. 'And finally, you will no longer lock us in.'

Shams pauses, then very slowly, very calmly says, 'If you don't cooperate, I will kill you.'

Shams knows what is rumoured about her in the camp. Not only is she supposedly responsible for Afifa's abduction, but she allegedly also killed her own father before the bomb dropped onto their house.

She pushes Omar's head down, putting her whole weight into her hands so that his face is pressed flat against the floor. After a while Omar begins to squirm beneath her, fighting for air. Nour has broken into sobs.

38

OMAR sticks to the rules. Shams helps Nour with the cooking and the little boy. She is biding her time.

Nour's second baby is born, another boy. Omar is pleased with himself and even forgets to be upset that Shams's period has come again.

39

EVERY day now, Shams goes to the market. She once more wears her colourful hijabs and her jeans and long-sleeved T-shirts. She smiles while she drives a hard bargain with the market vendors and greets each girl and each woman she knows without shyness or guilt.

40

SHAMS, *the poor girl, had nothing to do with the abduction.*

We all know it.

She is one of us.

She would never betray any of our girls.

Soon the whispers get louder, hissing through the alleyways – a hot desert storm tearing apart the rumours like a bundles of dry grass.

Shams has never done anyone any harm.

Poor girl, her entire family died in the rubble. The bombing was heavy that night.

They pulled her out half-dead.

She is right, only education will protect our girls from what happened to Afifa.

Umm Khalid tugs Shams's arm and pulls her into her home. Umm Khalid, who knew from the beginning that Shams was innocent. Who didn't believe the rumours. Who didn't want to go in front of the camera. No way, she didn't want to. But Abu Khalid threatened her with divorce. Honour demands revenge. The clan, scattered across the globe, had already begun to talk on various WhatsApp groups with mobile numbers from Syria and Canada and Germany and the US. Abu Khalid did not want to take revenge, he doesn't like bloodshed. And revenge, according to the clan, always has to do with bloodshed. So forcing Abu Ali to settle out of court on behalf of his niece appeared a sensible, non-violent solution to Abu Khalid. Yet Umm Khalid initially refused, told him to do it himself, going in front of the camera, if that's what he wanted. But of course he couldn't do it, that was beneath his dignity. It had to look as if Umm Khalid had acted on her own, so that a financial settlement would then seem like a good solution.

Later on, after her appearance in front of the camera, Umm Khalid had gone to Umm Ali. Umm Ali understood that Umm Khalid had had no choice. Divorce was worse than death. The two women cried and thanked God that Shams was now finally settled with Omar and that the distant cousin, the respectable, pious man who had come unexpectedly from Saudi and introduced Hassan to Afifa, had nothing to do with any of it.

And now Umm Khalid is tugging Shams's arm and pulling her into her home. If anyone chooses to ask her why she is doing it – to ask if she is finally courageous enough to say out loud what she has always known: that Shams is innocent – she wouldn't be able to answer.

She is obeying the rhythm of the flock.

And like a murmuration of blackbirds, the mothers in their black abayas are swooping into Umm Khalid's home. Umm Khalid herself, indeed, is following that very same flock with Shams in tow - each woman hurrying through the alleyways on the heels of her neighbour, feeling reassured that flocking offers safety in numbers, as it would be hard to pick out one single woman or girl to blame from among such a formation. No one has told them. No one person has decided. They all have decided. They are a swarm of mothers following their collective instinct, their synthetic abayas crinkling and crackling, producing little electric charges. There are too many of them by now who have tasted the benefits of what Shams used to offer their daughters. The mothers want more. They want Shams to continue teaching the girls. Because these daughters who used to be good for nothing have begun teaching their mothers how to say no to more children and how not to be cheated by market sellers and how to run the family budget. And the women like the control that this gives them over their lives.

No more time should be lost, they decide. And Shams's lessons start up again, taking place each day in someone else's home, very early in the morning, when husbands and uncles and teenage sons are still fast asleep.

41

AN almost complete silence travels up from the alleyways. Shatila's babies are all asleep, wrapped in sweet dreams. She feels her heart calming, her breathing slowing, the rushing in her ears subsiding. A soft, early morning breeze caresses her. Then, for a brief moment she has the impression that something is scurrying through her alleyways. It's shapeless. Not human, not animal. Like a fog, a nebulous wave in the light of dawn. Or a shoal of small fish at the bottom of the ocean on the move in one continuous, elongated, ever-changing wave.

Shatila sighs. Surely nothing to worry about. And she falls asleep.

AUTHOR'S NOTE

I used to live in leafy North London writing novels and managing a small publishing company, Peirene Press. However, I felt increasingly that my life lacked social impact. Was I doing anything really useful in the world? So, in 2018 my husband and I took the opportunity to spend a year working with Syrian refugees in Lebanon. I was excited to reactivate my Arabic, a language I had learnt at university.

During that year I met Kadria Hussien, a Syrian refugee woman living in Beirut. Together we began teaching a group of teenage girls from the Shatila refugee camp how to read and write. It was supposed to be a temporary set up. Kadria was waiting to receive refugee status to relocate to a Western country, while I was getting ready to go back to the UK. But then something happened that neither of us had foreseen. The girls began demanding more. 'We want a proper education,' they requested. 'We want the chance to go to school, we want to go to university.'

Lebanon is the country with the biggest pro capita refugee quota in the world. Every fourth person in Lebanon is a refugee. Of the 660,000 Syrian refugee children, 58% have never gone to school and 41% of the girls get married before the age of eighteen, many of them as early as twelve or thirteen years old. These are the official figures. Many marriages are unregistered, so the number is probably much higher.*

Kadria and I were aware that if we really wanted to respond to

* Sources: Save the Children 2023, Norwegian Refugee Council 2023, GirlsNot-Brides.

the request of the girls, we had to set up something with continuity in mind. So, in early 2020 we co-founded Alsama Project. With this came a conscious commitment by both of us. Kadria declined a chance to relocate with her family to Italy, I stepped down from the publishing house and moved to Beirut permanently.

Alsama means 'sky' in Arabic. We educate refugee children and empower refugee women in the Middle East.

The character of Shams is an amalgamation of the young women and girls I have been working with over the last six years in the Shatila refugee camp. These girls would have been married at the age of thirteen or fourteen if it weren't for their desire to receive an education. In many cases they are the first in their families to go to school. And they will also be among the first Alsama cohort to graduate in 2026. I have no doubt that some will go on to international universities. They want to study Business, Finance, and International Law. They want to build a life for their families, support their communities, contribute to Alsama, and eventually, return to rebuild Syria.

Shams is an expression of my deep admiration for these young people.

~

I am writing this at the beginning of October 2024. Only 10 days ago I sat with our top students in their classroom in Shatila and discussed *Why Nations Fail* by Daron Acemoglu & James Robinson.

Since then much has changed.

Over the last few days, the bombardment of Beirut has forced our students to flee war a second time in their short lives. Our schools are now closed and most of our staff and students are displaced. I wake up to the sound of bombing. My husband calls me every morning to see if I am OK.

Yet, as soon as they could the students were back in touch. 'We want to continue with Alsama. We have goals to achieve.'

We have begun to set up Alsama mini-centres outside the camps. We are buying Sim cards so that our students can participate in lessons online. We are renting apartments in less vulnerable areas to try to keep our students and our teachers safe.

Kadria's family – and my family – would like us to leave the country. We reassure them that we are safe.

'When war broke out in Syria, schools closed, never to reopen again,' Kadria told me. Education is always the first victim of armed conflict. Yet, we all know that it is only through teaching the next generation how to negotiate peacefully and seek compromises that we can work towards a better future.

Alsama was set up to provide education institutes for teenagers in regions blighted by armed conflict. It was inevitable that sooner or later Alsama would find itself operating in a war zone. This is not the time to give in. This is, in fact, an opportunity for Alsama to adapt, strengthen and continue.

I have always felt lucky to have been born in Europe at a time when I could chart my own course. Many are not so fortunate. I am passionate about helping people find their voices. Throughout my career I have achieved that through writing (first journalism, then fiction), setting up a publishing house that allowed me to publish foreign voices previously unheard of in English and now by running an organisation that saves refugee girls from early marriage and refugee boys from child labour. We do this by offering them a world-class education. As long as my presence can help them, I will stay.

All my earnings of this book will be donated to Alsama Project. www.alsamaproject.com

MEIKE ZIERVOGEL,
Beirut, 6th October 2024

This book has been typeset by
SALT PUBLISHING LIMITED
using Neacademia, a font designed by Sergei Egorov for the Rosetta Type Foundry in Czechia. It has been manufactured using Holmen Book Cream 65gsm paper, and printed and bound by Clays Limited in Bungay, Suffolk, Great Britain.

CROMER
GREAT BRITAIN
MMXXV